a feminine ending

by Sarah Treem

A SAMUEL FRENCH ACTING EDITION

SAMUEL FRENCH

FOUNDED 1830

New York Hollywood London Toronto

SAMUELFRENCH.COM

ISBN 9978-0-573-65235-6   Printed in U.S.A.   #8700

IMPORTANT BILLING AND CREDIT REQUIREMENTS

All producers of *A FEMININE ENDING must* give credit to the Author of the Play in all programs distributed in connection with performances of the Play, and in all instances in which the title of the Play appears for the purposes of advertising, publicizing or otherwise exploiting the Play and / or a production. The name of the Author *must* appear on a separate line on which no other name appears, immediately following the title and *must* appear in size of type not less than fifty percent of the size of the title type.

In addition the following credit *must* be given in all programs and publicity information distributed in association with this piece:

"Playwrights Horizons, Inc., New York City, produced the World Premiere
of A FEMININE ENDING Off-Broadway in 2007,
A FEMININE ENDING was originally developed at JAW; A Playwrights
Festival, Portland Center Stage, 2006"

A FEMININE ENDING premiered at Playwrights Horizons, Tim Sanford, Artistic Director, Leslie Marcus, Managing Director in October, 2007. The Stage Manager was Robyn Henry with sets by Cameron Anderson, costumes by Michael Krass, lighting by Ben Stanton, and sound by Obadiah Eaves. The production was directed by Blair Brown with the following cast:

JACK . . . . Alec Beard

AMANDA . . . . Gillian Jacobs

KIM . . . . Marsha Mason

DAVID . . . . Richard Masur

BILLY . . . . Joe Paulik

CHARACTERS

AMANDA, Mid 20s, oboist, aspiring composer.

JACK, Mid 20s, singer, up-and-coming pop star.

KIM, Early 50s, Amanda's mother. Homemaker.

DAVID, Early 50s, Amanda's father. Insurance salesman.

BILLY, Mid 20s, Postman.

SETTING

Amanda's house in Brooklyn. Her parents' house in New Hampshire. The recesses of her mind.

TIME

Present.

A note about Amanda: She is a character who hasn't quite found her voice. But she is not defeated. The actress playing her should fight against that choice. The internal conflict must be active.

A note about the scene titles: They should appear, somehow, on the set, between movements.

One last note: These people are not sentimentalists.

MOVEMENT ONE: MUSIC

Lights rise on a stage with nothing but a piano and a girl, named **AMANDA,** *down in front.*

AMANDA. It is known, by the few that know enough to care and care enough to know, that any piece of music has one of two beginnings. They are gendered. One is female. The other is male. Isn't that strange?

Lights fade down on **AMANDA** *and then rise again, instantly. Like a blink.*

AMANDA. I have become increasingly aware of the tyranny of gender. It's everywhere. We're obsessed with it. Men and women. Women and men. How they differ. How they fit. We don't use gender nouns in English. A door is just a door; it's not a girl or a boy door. That used to make me feel superior to French people. Now I envy them. If I had known, as a child, that EVERYTHING has a sex, I would not have wasted so much time trying to be a famous composer. Le compositeur. It doesn't have a feminine.

Lights down and up again. **AMANDA** *'s mother* **KIM,** *appears and hands her an oboe.*

AMANDA. But such information was deliberately withheld from me. My mother, who was too stoned to help out much during the feminist revolution, was nevertheless quite proud that it had occurred during the bloom of her youth. She insisted that I reap the benefits. By becoming something totally extraordinary.

KIM. Play the oboe. Nobody plays the oboe.

AMANDA. An oboist.

KIM exits. **AMANDA** *wets the reed. The lights go down and come up.*

AMANDA. There's a reason nobody plays the oboe. If played poorly –

AMANDA *blows a pitchless sound.*

AMANDA. – It sounds like a dying duck. But if played well –

AMANDA *plays a perfect A.*

AMANDA. It is the sound that tunes the entire orchestra. Strong and lonely. The instrument whose tonal quality best approximates a human voice. And it can't be tuned. There are no strings to tighten or gears to adjust. It cannot be anything other than it already is. It's like the Hamlet of instruments.

AMANDA *starts to play slowly. She stops herself.*

AMANDA. It is known, by the few that know enough to care and care enough to know, that any piece of music has one of two beginnings. They are gendered. A masculine piece begins with an emphasis or "stress" on the first beat. A feminine piece begins with the "stress" on the second beat. Or sometimes, the third.

This is a feminine beginning.

Enter **JACK**. *They smile at each other. He takes the oboe and exits.*

AMANDA. Gorgeous, isn't he? That's Jack Handel. If you haven't heard of him yet – you're about to. He's going to be "huge". Everyone says so.

JACK *starts bringing on the furniture of their apartment. He sets it up behind* **AMANDA** *as she speaks.*

AMANDA. We met in New York City. We were both getting our graduate degrees in music. I had become a composer. That's a common progression for a career oboist. Because we tune the orchestra we begin to think symphonically very early on.

Jack was a year behind me, majoring in voice.

There's a club in the basement of the university and on Tuesdays they have an open mic night. I used to go sometimes and play my latest compositions. Jack would always be there, singing.

JACK, who has finished setting up the bedroom, takes a spotlight, downstage left, and sings something to the audience.

AMANDA. He has this way of convincing every person in the audience that he is singing directly to them. His manager, Hillary, calls it "star quality". She says that's what separates Jack from the people who sing in subways.

Hillary says star quality boils down to whether or not a normal person thinks you would sleep with them. Hillary says the quality manifests itself differently in men and women. Female stars need to be warm and inviting and it helps if they seem a little confused. Or slightly depressed. But the male star must make each woman believe he would choose her from a crowd to seduce. So he can't be depressed at all. A woman has to see her future in his eyes. Hillary says this is because men want to fuck and run and woman want to submit and be kept. Before Hillary became a manager, she wrote self-help books for single women. And that, according to Jack, is what makes her the best in the business.

JACK stops singing and approaches AMANDA.

JACK. Hey.

AMANDA. Hey.

JACK. I really enjoyed your piece tonight.

AMANDA. Really?

JACK. I was thinking - we should collaborate on something.

AMANDA. That would be great! I'm working on a woodwind quartet right now but I could totally change the oboe to voice.

JACK. Why don't we start with something a little easier?

AMANDA. Like what?

JACK. Like this.

(JACK kisses AMANDA)

AMANDA. See, for me, the quartet is easier.

JACK kisses AMANDA again and moves her back upstage. They fall on the bed, kissing. Lights down.

MOVEMENT TWO: FAME

The lights come up again, suddenly. **JACK** *is sleeping.* **AMANDA** *is sitting up, with the covers pulled around her.*

AMANDA. (*a conspiracy with the audience*) Before I knew it, I was Jack Handel's girlfriend. And suddenly I was the target of unmitigated resentment from every hipless hipster below fourteenth street. Because anybody who was anybody in the know already knew that Jack Handel was about to be huge.

JACK *snores loudly and turns over.*

AMANDA *sneaks quietly out of bed, wrapped in the bed-sheet, and sits down at her piano. She puts her hands on the keyboard, then turns back to the audience.*

AMANDA. In the moments he isn't singing, Jack is a hot mess. But I like that about him. Taking care of him makes me feel strong. Competent. Like a woman. Well, like my mother anyway.

At night, we lie in bed together, hands clasped and talk about how to activate our potential.

Jack sleeps with earplugs because I get all my best ideas in my dreams.

She turns to the piano. She turns back to the audience.

AMANDA. There's this song I want to write. I've been hearing it my whole life in my head. It goes like this…

She turns to the piano. Puts her hands on the keyboard. Turns back.

AMANDA. It begins with the sound of snow melting on the roof of the house I grew up in and dripping slowly from the gutter into tin pails…

AMANDA *plays some very high, tin-sounding notes.*

AMANDA. And then the frogs that live in the tin pails awaken…

AMANDA *plays some low, croaking chords.*

AMANDA. The front door opens with the first burst of sun, and then …

AMANDA*'s fingers float over the keyboard.*

AMANDA. And then…

AMANDA *gets lost in the moment of composition. She doesn't know the chord.*

AMANDA. And then…

AMANDA *slowly, softly begins to play Chopin's very recognizable Nocturne No. 2 in E-flat.* JACK *wakes up. He sits up in bed. Takes the earplugs out of his ears.*

JACK. Did you write that?

AMANDA *shakes her head.*

AMANDA. Chopin.

JACK. Huh. He sounds like you.

AMANDA. Did I wake you? I'm sorry.

JACK. It's okay. I was having a nightmare. I was famous.

AMANDA *nods. She keeps playing.*

JACK. Everyone around me had beaks instead of noses.

AMANDA *keeps playing.*

JACK. Will you still love me when I'm famous?

AMANDA *stops.*

JACK. Why'd you stop?

AMANDA. You make it sound inevitable.

JACK. You just have to trust that life has a road mapped out for you.

AMANDA. Is that from your Celebrity Quotes Calendar?

JACK. Yes.

AMANDA. Who said it?

JACK. Orlando Bloom.

Beat.

AMANDA *smiles. She turns back to the piano and plays a few measures.*

JACK. I like Chopin.

AMANDA. This stuff is mine.

JACK. How's the symphony coming?

AMANDA. It's coming.

JACK. I can't wait to hear it.

AMANDA. Neither can I.

AMANDA *sighs. Frustrated.*

JACK. It's clearly time for my secret symphony-summoning dance.

AMANDA. Your what?

JACK. Go ahead. Start playing.

AMANDA *starts playing the beginning of her symphony.* **JACK** *starts to dance, silly but joyously.*

JACK. Keep playing. I think it's working.

AMANDA *shakes her head.* **JACK** *stops dancing.*

AMANDA. You amaze me.

JACK. Come back to bed and I'll really knock your socks off.

AMANDA *gets back in the bed.*

AMANDA. I have something to tell you

JACK. I have something to tell you. You go first.

AMANDA. I got offered a job. Composing.

JACK. Baby! For which orchestra?

AMANDA. Jingles. For an advertising firm.

JACK. Oh. Hey that's something.

AMANDA. It's money.

JACK. Money is good.

AMANDA. I need to make a living Jack.

JACK. I know.

AMANDA. Not everyone has a trust fund.

JACK. Wow. Okay. Hey, bite me.

> **JACK** *turns his back on her and rolls over. Furious.*

AMANDA. I'm sorry.

JACK. You should be. That money keeps my whole family shackled to my father. He tells my sister who to marry. He tells my mother what medication to take.

AMANDA. I know.

JACK. He tells me that after I get this music thing out of my system, I'm going to business school.

AMANDA. I know. I know.

JACK. No, you don't, because you've got these provincial little parents who think you're a genius.

AMANDA. What was your news?

JACK. What?

AMANDA. You said you had something to tell me.

JACK. Oh. I got a manager. Her name is Hillary. She represents Nick Lachey.*

AMANDA. Are you serious?

JACK. Yeah.

AMANDA. Jack!

JACK. What?

AMANDA. That's great.

JACK. She thinks I should quit school and concentrate.

AMANDA. Are you going to do it?

JACK. I don't know. I was going to ask you what I should do. Before I got angry at you. Now I don't know who to ask.

AMANDA. I think you should do it.

JACK. You do?

AMANDA. Absolutely.

JACK. My father will disown me.

AMANDA. Who cares?

---

* If Nick Lachey is no longer relevant, substitute the name of a new B-list popstar.

JACK. He'll stop sending me an allowance.

AMANDA. I have money. I write advertising jingles.

JACK. No –

AMANDA. I can pay the rent for a while.

JACK. No! I didn't mean – I just wanted to know if you thought it was a good idea.

AMANDA. It's a great idea. You have to do it.

JACK. You're not paying my rent –

AMANDA. It will only be for a little while –

JACK. It might take longer.

AMANDA. Jack Handel. You are going to be huge. Everyone says so.

JACK. And then I'll pay for you.

AMANDA. Deal.

They grin at each other.

JACK. You and I are going to have an extraordinary life.

AMANDA. Will we be mad with happiness?

JACK. I won't be.

AMANDA. Why not?

JACK. It's not in my nature. I will have a horizon pool, however.

AMANDA. I want to be happy.

JACK. I can't promise you that. I can only promise you a horizon pool and an extraordinary life.

JACK's phone starts to ring. He picks it up.

JACK. *(surprised.)* It's Hillary.

JACK heads off the stage.

AMANDA. *(to the audience)* I know what you're thinking. You don't have to say it. My mother already did.

KIM, enters with a phone. AMANDA picks up a phone in her bedroom and holds the receiver directly out towards the audience. The sound echoes through the theatre.

KIM. ARE YOU INSANE?!

AMANDA. (*into the receiver*) I don't think so. Why?

AMANDA holds the receiver back out.

KIM. They have organizations for people who want to throw their money away, Amanda. They're called charities.

AMANDA. (*into the receiver*) I'm not throwing my money away.

KIM. You're not?

AMANDA. No. Jack is, like, an investment.

KIM. Mutual funds are, like, investments. Aspiring musicians in New York are like garbage disposals.

JACK. Baby?

JACK enters, holding something behind his back. He's trying to get AMANDA's attention.

AMANDA. Mom, I gotta go.

KIM. What about your music, Amanda? When are you going to work on that?

AMANDA. I'm working on it.

KIM. When was the last time you finished a piece?

AMANDA. I'm working on a symphony. They take a while.

JACK grows impatient.

AMANDA. I'll call you back, okay?

KIM. You're throwing your life away – all your god-given talent – on a good-for-nothing –

AMANDA. I love you too –

KIM. Amanda, I have to talk to you. It's about your father –

AMANDA. Give my love to Daddy. Bye.

AMANDA hangs up the phone.

JACK. I got you a Christmas present.

AMANDA. It's a little early.

JACK. I couldn't wait.

JACK pulls a ring box from behind his back.

JACK. Will you marry me, Amanda Blue?

AMANDA. Did you steal that?

JACK. I bought it.

AMANDA. With what?

JACK. Money.

AMANDA. Your father's money?

JACK. I signed.

AMANDA. You what?

JACK. I signed. *I signed.* With Virgin records, baby. I'm going to cut an album!

AMANDA. You signed?! When?

JACK. This afternoon. Hillary sent my demo to Virgin. They called me into their offices and asked me all about myself. I told them about me and a little about you and we signed a contract and then they gave me money to buy you something nice. I was gonna get you a new oboe, but then I thought about this.

Beat.

What do you think?

AMANDA. I don't know what to say.

JACK. Will you wear it?

AMANDA. I'll wear it.

JACK. You'll wear it? Then you like it?

AMANDA. I do.

They kiss.

AMANDA. I have to call my mother. I have to tell her.

JACK. Okay, call your mother. I'm gonna call my manager.

JACK *exits.*

AMANDA *picks up the phone.*

Lights back up on **KIM***'s phone. It rings.* **KIM** *rushes on to answer it.*

KIM. Hello?

AMANDA. Mom?

KIM. Oh Amanda, thank god. Your father is in the other room, so I can't talk too loudly –

AMANDA. I'm getting married!

KIM stops. Holds the phone out. Stares at it.

AMANDA. Can you hear me? Hello?

KIM hangs up the phone and walks offstage, out of the light.

AMANDA. Mom?

JACK reenters.

JACK. Hillary said nobody likes a married rock star. She wants to know if we'd consider having a baby out of wedlock instead.

AMANDA. You told her no, right?

JACK takes out his phone. Presses a number. Smiles at **AMANDA**.

JACK. (*Into the phone*) Hi, Hillary, it's Jack. Ah … she says no.

JACK hangs up the phone. Off **AMANDA**'s *look* –

JACK. I hate saying no to my manager.

AMANDA takes off her ring.

JACK. Oh no, don't do that. Why are you doing that? Listen, this is all new to me. I don't know how to behave. There seem to be these rules – but no one tells you what they are – and I don't want to piss anybody off. Not just for me – for you as well. I'm trying to build us a life, an extraordinary life.

AMANDA puts the ring back on.

A mail slot in the door opens up and a thick envelope falls through.

JACK. How long have we been talking like this?

AMANDA. About four months.

JACK. Shit.

> **JACK** *rushes off stage.*
>
> *Somewhere on set, a projection flashes "Four Months Later" then disappears.*

AMANDA. Last summer, I finished a concerto that I was particularly proud of and submitted it for consideration in the New York Symphonique's Spring New Voices festival. A month ago, I got a letter saying it had been chosen as a finalist. Now the New York Symphonique is not the Philharmonic but it is a New York orchestra and a good one. A concerto at the spring festival would launch my career. The finalists are supposed to submit a personal statement. All I've got down so far is "Please pick me." It was due last week.

> **JACK** *bursts through the door, and picks up the package.*

JACK. Hey.

AMANDA. Hey.

JACK. You got a package.

> *He hands* **AMANDA** *the package. She looks at the address.*

AMANDA. Who's Katrina?

JACK. What are you doing?

AMANDA. Writing my personal –

JACK. Want to go out to dinner with the President of Virgin?

AMANDA. As in Records? Sure! When?

JACK. Right now. In fact, we're late.

AMANDA. Wait, what?

JACK. I'm sorry – I meant to call you earlier but the day went by so quick.

AMANDA. But I have to write this statement of interest tonight.

JACK. You haven't done that yet?

AMANDA. When was I supposed to do it? I haven't even worked on my symphony in weeks. I'm, like, eight jingles behind. The house is a disaster. I have a wedding to plan –

JACK. I didn't realize planning a wedding would be such a chore –

AMANDA. Of course you didn't. Because you haven't helped with any of it.

Beat.

JACK. It is not my fault you're not composing. There's the goddamn piano.

AMANDA *turns away from him. She rips open her package.*

JACK. Amanda, I'm sorry. Can't you just come out to dinner now and hate me later?

Beat. No response.

Who is that from?

AMANDA. One of your fans.

JACK. You're opening my fan mail now?

AMANDA. It was addressed to me.

JACK. Give me that!

AMANDA *hands* **JACK** *the package. He looks inside and recoils at its contents.*

JACK. What is that?

AMANDA. It's a bloody tampon.

JACK. This – this is sick.

AMANDA. (*handing Jack the letter*) And a death threat.

JACK. (*reading*) Hillary said this might happen if I announced my engagement. It's a good sign. It means I'm developing a loyal fan base. They don't want me to get married. You should probably just stop opening the mail.

AMANDA *looks at* **JACK** *like "you've got to be kidding* *me".*

JACK. I'll talk to her, okay. I'm sorry. And I'm *tired* of being sorry. Can't you try a little harder to understand what I'm going through? I'm scared, baby. What if my album is terrible? What if nobody buys it? I dropped out of school. I have nothing to fall back on.

The telephone rings. AMANDA *and* JACK *look at each other.*

AMANDA. It's not for me.

JACK. Will you get dressed?

AMANDA. Fine.

Amanda heads offstage.

JACK *picks up the phone.*

JACK. Hello?

AMANDA. *(referencing the letter)* If it's Katrina, tell her "cease" is spelled with one s and "desist" is spelled with two.

JACK. It's your mother.

AMANDA *takes the phone from* JACK. JACK *points to his watch and mouths "five minutes". She nods. He takes the bloody tampon and letter offstage.*

AMANDA. Hi Mom.

Spotlight up on KIM, *talking on the phone downstage.*

KIM. What are you doing?

AMANDA. Right now? I'm talking to you.

KIM. Can you come home?

AMANDA. To New Hampshire?

KIM. Are you free?

AMANDA. When?

KIM. Now.

AMANDA. What's the matter?

KIM. I need your help with something.

AMANDA. What?

KIM. I can't tell you about it over the phone –

AMANDA. Is it illegal?

KIM. Hold on a second, your father's just leaving –

AMANDA. Where's he going?

KIM. He has a conference this weekend in Toronto – (*calling offstage*) David, dear, you better go outside – the taxi will be here any moment.

Amanda's father, **DAVID***, appears down stage right, with a suitcase in his hand. He looks tired.*

DAVID. Aren't you going to kiss me good-bye?

KIM. I can't darling, I'm on the phone with your daughter. She's having a breakdown.

AMANDA. No I'm not!

KIM. (*to* **DAVID**) I'll blow you a kiss from here.

KIM *blows* **DAVID** *a kiss. He watches it fly past his shoulder.*

DAVID. I missed.

DAVID *and his suitcase open the door and exit.*

KIM. Are you coming or not?

AMANDA. Who me?

KIM. Yes or no, Mandy. Say yes.

JACK *re-enters. He points to his watch.*

AMANDA. You can't give me a clue as to what this is all about?

KIM. Amanda, there comes a time in every young woman's life where she must take a giant step forward into the abyss we call maturity and acknowledge the painful, terrifying truth that her mother is a human being.

AMANDA. I know you're human, Mom.

KIM. Are you coming or not?

AMANDA. Of course, if you need me to come, I'll come –

KIM. Good. Leave now. I'll start dinner.

KIM *hangs up the phone. Lights down on* KIM.

JACK. What's up?

AMANDA. That was my mother.

JACK. She hates me.

AMANDA. She doesn't hate you.

JACK. Yes she does. It doesn't matter. In a few years, I'll be financing her retirement, so she'll have to be nice to my face. She wants you to go somewhere?

AMANDA. Yes. Home.

JACK. When?

AMANDA. Tonight.

JACK. Why?

AMANDA. I think something's wrong.

JACK. What?

AMANDA. She wouldn't tell me.

JACK. You told her you'd come?

AMANDA. I said, if she needed me –

JACK. What about dinner?

AMANDA. I… I'll call her back.

JACK. Your mom is fine. She's just lonely. And she knows she can call you up and get you to drop everything because she breastfed you guilt milk. You're a twenty-five year old woman! You're getting married. Call her back and tell her you have a commitment this week-end but you would be happy to visit her sometime next week. Okay?

AMANDA. Okay Jack.

JACK. The limo will be here in three minutes to pick us up.

The phone rings again. AMANDA *answers it.*

AMANDA. Mom?

Beat.

It's Hillary.

AMANDA *hands the phone to* JACK *and goes offstage to change.*

JACK. Hey Hil.

Yeah, I'm all ready to go.

No, I parted it a little off-center, like we talked about.

Yeah, I think it opens up my face too. Amanda's just changing.

Amanda, she's –

Oh, she isn't? But I thought he said I should bring a –

Oh. *Oh.*

No, that's great.

No, I understand.

Yeah, no problem. See you soon. Bye.

AMANDA *reenters, looking lovely, in a little black dress and heels. She's putting on earrings.*

AMANDA. Is this okay?

JACK. You look amazing.

AMANDA. I'm excited. Oh, I have to call my mom back –

She reaches for the phone. He stops her.

JACK. I – I fucked up. Hillary. Invited herself. To go with me. Tonight.

AMANDA. As your date?

JACK. No, it's a business dinner, really. They say bring a "date" but you're supposed to bring your manager. Everyone knows that apparently. Except me.

The apartment buzzer buzzes.

JACK. That's her now. I'm sorry.

AMANDA. That's okay.

JACK. I won't stay out late.

AMANDA. Take your time. I have to write my personal statement –

JACK. Please don't go to New Hampshire tonight.

A slight beat.

AMANDA. Okay.

JACK. We'll talk about everything when I get home.

AMANDA. Sure.

The buzzer buzzes again.

JACK. We are "this" close to an extraordinary life.

AMANDA. Jack, go.

JACK. I love you.

JACK kisses her and leaves.

AMANDA picks up the telephone.

Light up on KIM's phone, ringing. KIM enters and picks it up.

KIM. Hello?

AMANDA. I'm on my way.

Lights down.

MOVEMENT THREE: MARRIAGE

As **JACK** *and* **DAVID** *take off the furniture of the New York apartment and bring on the furniture of the New Hampshire house, Amanda moves back downstage and addresses the audience.*

AMANDA. (*direct address*) When I was a girl, around twelve or so – I wanted to write an opera. I knew that Mozart had done it even earlier and he was a boy, so I figured it couldn't be that hard.

Operas are about love but at twelve the only person I truly loved was my mother. I thought she was terrific. So I decided to write an opera about her.

When I was young I heard harmony everywhere. The garbage truck harmonized with the lawn mower. The dishwasher harmonized with the air conditioner. My mother harmonized with my father. Their harmony was the most beautiful. Intricate but effortless. Even when they argued. It's all about balance. One voice, one strand, compliments the other through contradiction. So when my mother hits a series of rapid sliding high notes like:

KIM *enters and speaks to the audience.*

KIM. "Davidwhatdoyouthinkyourdoing?Youcannotinviteyo urbossoverfordinnertonightwehavenofoodinthehouse andthere'sablizzardcomingandbesidesdoIlooklikeyou rmothertoyou?"

AMANDA. My father would interject low, staccato notes at punctuating intervals like:

DAVID *stops whatever he's doing, puts down whatever he's lifting, and faces* **KIM**.

KIM. "Davidwhatdoyouthinkyourdoing?/Youcannotinvitey-ourbossoverfordinnertonightwehavenofoodinthehou-seandtheresablizzardcomingandbesidesdoIlooklikey-ourmothertoyou?"

DAVID. (*intercutting Kim's diatribe*) "I thought – Alright – I'll call – Kim – Enough!"

AMANDA. And they'd be harmonizing.

DAVID and KIM glare at each other.

AMANDA. And sometimes, when you least expected it, they'd come back together, at the height of the interval, so completely you would think there had been only one simple melody all along. One voice. No partition.

KIM AND DAVID. I heard you!

KIM and DAVID exit.

Lights shift. **AMANDA** *turns and suddenly, she's in the house in New Hampshire. The room is lit by candlelight. It's decorated "colonially" with wooden figurines and hand-dipped candles, family pictures on the mantle and a piano in the corner.*

In the center of the room, by candlelight, **KIM** *is packing a suitcase very carefully, ritualistically, laying tissue paper in layers between the articles of clothing.*

AMANDA. (*softly*) Mom?

KIM looks up. Gasps.

KIM. Why didn't you knock?

AMANDA. The lights were out. I didn't think anyone was home.

KIM. Good. That's the point, isn't it?

AMANDA. What's the point, Mom?

KIM. Vacancy. Abandonment. It would be pointless to knock. Or stop in for a chat. We are, so very clearly, not at home.

AMANDA. You want people to think you've gone away?

KIM. I must be left alone to work in peace. Did anyone see you come in? Does anyone know you're here?

AMANDA. Jack knows where I am.

KIM. Who?

AMANDA. Jack, Mom, you know Jack. My fiancée.

KIM. Jack. Yes. You're still seeing him, I gather?

AMANDA. We're engaged Mom.

KIM. Oh don't say that.

AMANDA. Why don't you like him? He's a really good guy.

KIM. He's unbearably formal.

AMANDA. You make him nervous!

KIM. I don't make anyone nervous. Not even squirrels.

AMANDA. Squirrels?

KIM. They don't find me intimidating. Not in the least. Everyone else – they're afraid of. Your father looks in their direction and they scatter. But me, I'll be walking down the road, and there, right in the middle of the path, two squirrels will be having an argument –

AMANDA. An argument?

KIM. A discussion. A conversation. *Whatever.* The point is, they don't move. Not even when I'm half a foot away from them. Not even if I step over them. They stay right where they are. As if I wasn't even there. As if I didn't even exist. I have become invisible.

AMANDA. No, Mom, you're just in a rut –

KIM. Do not pity me. I'm not seeking sympathy. It was a deliberate choice. Phase one.

AMANDA. Phase one?

KIM. Are you aware that you're repeating everything I say?

AMANDA. What are you talking about?!

KIM. You just said "phase one", after I did. Earlier you said "Squirrels"? And then "an argument"? You're trying to belittle me. But it won't work. I'm determined to do it.

AMANDA. Determined to do it?

KIM. There you go again –

AMANDA. What are you determined to do?

Beat.

KIM. Leave your father, of course.

>AMANDA *sits down. She is suddenly very, very tired.*

AMANDA. Of course.

KIM. You just did it again!

AMANDA. When?

KIM. This weekend.

AMANDA. That's why you needed me to come up.

KIM. To help me pack. We need to be gone by the time your father comes home.

AMANDA. Which is?

KIM. Tomorrow night.

>*Pause.*

KIM. That's plenty of time, Amanda.

>*No response.*

KIM. At school, some of my students snort Ritalin when they have to stay up all night to study. They gave me some, in powder form. Ground it right there in front of me.

>KIM *takes some white powder out of her purse to show* AMANDA.

KIM. Is that what cocaine looks like?

AMANDA. I don't know, Mom. I don't do coke.

KIM. Still, now that Jack's a rockstar, you must be exposed to it.

AMANDA. He's not a rockstar.

KIM. That's not what my students say.

AMANDA. Your students are talking about Jack?

KIM. The ones that snort Ritalin are. They somehow found his webpage and saw he had dedicated some songs to Amanda Blue. They only wanted to know if you and I were related. I gave them your address. They wanted to send him something to sign.

AMANDA. Mom, do you have a student named Katrina?

KIM. Yes, actually.

AMANDA. Don't give my address out anymore, okay?

KIM. Why? Did she send a letter?

AMANDA. It's just not a good idea.

KIM. Are you hungry? I made tuna melts.

AMANDA. Mom, I –

KIM. Thank you so much for coming, Mandy. You can't possibly imagine what it means. It's times like these when I remember why I had a daughter. (*Beat*) That didn't come out right.

AMANDA. Don't thank me. You know I'm leaving.

KIM. You just got here.

AMANDA. And I realize I made a mistake. So I'm leaving.

KIM. I think somebody's a little cranky. I think somebody could use a tuna melt –

AMANDA. I have a wedding to plan Mom. I have a job. I have a life back in New York that I cannot believe I let you coax me away from because Dad is gone for the weekend and you're feeling lonely.

Beat.

KIM. I'm leaving your father, Amanda.

AMANDA. Like hell you are.

KIM. Why do you think I've packed this suitcase?

AMANDA. Because you're bored and you're looking for a fantasy to entertain. This isn't the first time you've done this. Remember Nantucket?

KIM. That was different.

AMANDA. How was that different?

KIM. I didn't go through with it then.

AMANDA. And you're not going to go through with it now. We're going race around the house all weekend, in the dark apparently, packing up the silver and the china and the linens –

KIM. I'm leaving the linens. They're hideous. They belonged to his mother –

AMANDA. And you're going to change your mind at the

very last moment, right before Daddy comes back, and shove everything into the closet and we're all going to have dinner tomorrow night as if nothing ever happened.

KIM. It's different this time.

AMANDA. It took me a year to look Daddy in the eye again after Nantucket.

KIM. You always were such a ridiculously sensitive child –

AMANDA. You told me he was a bad man –

KIM. You were ten. Was I supposed to tell you your father hadn't fucked me in a year?

Beat.

AMANDA. No!

KIM. Well, what should I have done? Left you there? If you hadn't thrown such a tempertantrum we might have made that ferry.

Beat.

AMANDA. I'll make it easier for you this time. I'll get out of your way now.

AMANDA *gets up and grabs her coat.*

KIM. This time I have proof.

AMANDA *stops.*

AMANDA. What kind of proof?

KIM. Hold on. Just hold on.

KIM *exits into the kitchen and comes back with a small package of tinfoil. She hands it to* **AMANDA.**

AMANDA. What is this?

KIM. Open it and see.

AMANDA. Why is it cold?

KIM. It was in the refrigerator.

AMANDA *pulls out a pair of hot pink, lacey women's panties.*

AMANDA. What are these?

KIM. They look like panties to me.

AMANDA. Whose panties?

KIM. I couldn't tell you, darling. I could only make an educated guess. I found them in your father's coat pocket.

AMANDA. Did you ask him what he's doing with them?

KIM. No, I didn't.

AMANDA. Why not?

KIM. Because I don't particularly want to know what he's doing with them or to whom they belong. I just want to leave him.

> **AMANDA** *hands the panties back to* **KIM**.

AMANDA. What are you waiting for?

KIM. You think I should do it?

AMANDA. You don't need my permission –

KIM. But I do need your key.

AMANDA. What key?

KIM. I need some place to stay, just for a few months, until I find a job.

AMANDA. No.

KIM. Aman –

AMANDA. No! No! No! No! This has gone far enough. You can't move in.

KIM. It wouldn't be for very long –

AMANDA. You said a few months –

KIM. You lived in my house for eighteen years, Amanda. Time is relative.

AMANDA. I'm getting married –

KIM. I've done that before – I can help.

AMANDA. I don't want your help.

KIM. Fine, then I won't help. I won't even talk to you. I'll talk to Jack.

AMANDA. Jack's never home.

KIM. Is he having an affair?

AMANDA. No! He's – I don't know – he got meetings and – photo shoots. They're so excited about his album, they pushed up the release date. Which is why we had to change the wedding day.

KIM. You've changed the wedding day?

AMANDA. We sent out those change-the-date cards –

KIM. I never got a card.

AMANDA. Are you sure?

KIM. You'll only be the first Mrs. Handel. You do understand that, don't you? Famous people never stay with their first wives. Let Jack marry somebody else this time around. You can pick him up again in five or six years. Hey, where are you going?

AMANDA is heading out the door.

AMANDA. It's been a pleasure Mother, as usual.

KIM. Wait, you can't leave –

AMANDA. Yes, I can – that's the beauty of being financially independent.

KIM. I don't even know the date of your new wedding.

AMANDA. Look on your changed-the-date card.

KIM. I threw it out. I thought it was junk mail.

AMANDA. February 16th.

KIM. Oh honey, your father and I are planning a trip for February –

Beat.

But now that I'm leaving him – I can come.

Beat.

AMANDA. I'll tell the caterer.

KIM. I'm sorry about what I said.

AMANDA. Which part?

KIM. About you being Jack's first wife. I don't know that. I don't know anything.

AMANDA. It's fine.

KIM. I just want you to be happy. I don't want to see you get hurt. I don't want you to end up here, in this place, after thirty years.

> **KIM** *hangs her head and sniffs.* **AMANDA** *waits, impassive.*

KIM. Can't you see that I'm upset?

AMANDA. I'm waiting.

KIM. For what, Armageddon?

AMANDA. For tears.

> **AMANDA** *walks over to her mother and looks into her eyes.*

AMANDA. That's what I thought. Good luck packing. If you actually make it to New York, call me from there –

KIM. Amanda! AMANDA!

> **AMANDA** *walks out the front door and slams it behind her. The scene in the house immediately goes dark. A light snow starts down.*

> **AMANDA** *looks at the audience. She's startled by their presence. And a little embarrassed.*

AMANDA. Sorry, where were we? Right, my first opera. The one inspired by my mother.

When I sat down to write the glory of my mother, I could not seem to keep her voice far enough away from mine. The notes came out too close to harmonize, though not close enough to synchronize. If my voice came in on A, I would hear her voice, right above me, on A sharp, riding my thread. Every time my voice chose a new direction, her voice would follow the same course but a half-step above or below – as if she was *correcting me.* Harmonize, I commanded myself. Make them harmonize. But no matter what I did, I could not get the two voices *to listen to each other.*

I gave up on opera after that.

AMANDA *walks over to a place downstage where her "car" is parked and mimes getting in.*

AMANDA. I'm going home. If you're wondering what I'm doing. This is my car.

AMANDA *mimes turning the car on, putting it into gear and backing out of the driveway.*

BILLY *enters, behind her, dressed in his postal uniform, distributing mail.*

AMANDA *mimes stopping short. The sound of a car skidding.*

BILLY, *jumps out of the way.*

AMANDA. (*to the audience*) That's the postman. (*To* BILLY) I'm sorry. Are you okay?

BILLY. Amanda Blue?

AMANDA. Billy Theebles?

BILLY THEEBLES *freezes.*

AMANDA. (*to the audience*) Billy Theebles was my first kiss. It happened right here, actually. Ten years ago. On this very patch of land.

AMANDA. So how've you been?

BILLY *unfreezes.*

BILLY. Can't complain. What about you? Visiting the folks?

AMANDA. My mom asked me to come up for the weekend –

BILLY. You're around all weekend?

AMANDA. No, I'm heading home tonight.

BILLY. Oh, well … why?

AMANDA. I've got a lot to do –

Beat.

I'm getting married.

BILLY. Who is the lucky guy? Do I know him?

AMANDA. You might.

BILLY. Someone from high school?

AMANDA. No, he's ... he's sort of famous. He's about to be famous.

BILLY. Is he a suicide bomber?

AMANDA. No!

BILLY. Would he tell you if he was?

AMANDA. He's a singer. He's been signed by a major record label.

BILLY. Is he very good-looking?

AMANDA. (*surprised*) Yes.

BILLY. Then he'll go far.

AMANDA. He's talented too.

BILLY. Writes his own songs?

AMANDA. No. Vocally. He sings like an angel.

BILLY. I won't buy his album.

AMANDA. He'll be crushed.

BILLY. I don't respect artists with nothing original to say.

A very bizarre beat.

AMANDA. Okay. It was nice to see you again. I have to get on the road.

BILLY. Have you been signed with a major record label?

AMANDA. Not quite.

BILLY. Is that hard on your relationship?

AMANDA. Would you mind moving? I don't want to hit you.

BILLY. I'm done with my mail route. Just finished.

AMANDA. It's two o'clock in the morning.

BILLY. I like to start in the evening. It's cooler.

AMANDA. But this is November.

BILLY. Also, in the evenings, there are people in the windows. Of the houses. So that's exciting.

Beat.

AMANDA. That's voyeurism.

BILLY. Wow, you've really become a glass-half-empty kind of girl.

AMANDA *just stares at him.*

BILLY. Did you know this is the very last house on my route?

AMANDA *looks around.*

AMANDA. It's in the middle of the street.

BILLY. Yes, but I start with the house next door.

BILLY *and* **AMANDA** *look over at the house next door.*

AMANDA. Why?

BILLY. That's just what I do. Also I live there.

AMANDA. Since when?

BILLY. Since I bought it.

AMANDA. You bought the house next door to my parents?

BILLY. Is this your parents' house? I had no idea.

AMANDA. You just asked me if I was home visiting my parents.

BILLY. Okay, fine, I had a hunch.

AMANDA. Billy? Were you always this strange?

BILLY. I was. You used to be strange too.

AMANDA. Hardly.

BILLY. In high school, whenever one of the popular boys would ask you out, you'd look them straight in the eye and say "Sing A".

AMANDA. I never did that –

BILLY. The only reason you agreed to go out with me is because I told you I had perfect pitch.

AMANDA. Do you have perfect pitch?

BILLY. (*with a smirk*) Yes I do.

AMANDA. Sing A.

BILLY *sings something that is definitely not A and might not even be considered a note.* **AMANDA** *smiles.*

AMANDA. It was nice to see you.

BILLY. It was nice to see you too.

AMANDA. I really need to be getting back to the city now.

BILLY. No you don't.

AMANDA. I can't imagine how you'd know that.

BILLY. Doesn't your fiancée have a photo-shoot or something? Come out with me tonight.

AMANDA. With you?

BILLY. Come on. A night on the town. For old times sake.

AMANDA. What town?

BILLY. What town, she scoffs. See, Amanda Blue, this is what people like you don't understand – people who move away after high school. They don't understand that there are adults living in this town as well as under-aged teenagers, and that these said adults have places where they go to drink –

AMANDA. I'm flattered Billy, really, but –

BILLY. Come on, and tomorrow you can go back to your soft-rock, easy-listening fiancée and get married with no regrets – absolutely certain that you did not leave the love of your life, freezing his cojones off in your parents' driveway in some sleepy little town somewhere halfway to nowhere. How's that for security?

AMANDA wavers. BILLY leans in and kisses her. She raises her hand to slap him. He catches it.

BILLY. Go ahead.

BILLY releases her hand. AMANDA slaps him, hard.

BILLY. Jiminy Cricket!

AMANDA. Are you okay?

BILLY. Not really.

AMANDA. Good.

AMANDA leaves BILLY downstage and walks back upstage and into her house. The lights come up. KIM is carefully rewrapping the incriminating underwear in tinfoil.

AMANDA drops her bags.

AMANDA. I'm staying.

Before **KIM** *can respond,* **AMANDA** *turns on her heels and walks out. The lights go off in the house.*

AMANDA *returns to* **BILLY**, *shivering outside.*

AMANDA. How are your cojones?
BILLY. Shrunken.

BILLY *heads offstage.* **AMANDA** *starts to follow him, then turns back to the audience.*

AMANDA. I'm acting as if I'd forgotten all about Billy but I'm lying. I think about him a lot. More than I'd like too. We were together almost constantly when we were young. It took him years to work up the courage to kiss me. He used to show up at my house in the evenings and ask me if I wanted to go for a walk and "clear my head." We'd go wandering around the neighborhoods and we'd stop under every street lamp and he'd look at me, mournfully. Finally, after our eighty-third stroll, I said "Billy are you going to kiss me or not?" And he said "I was thinking about it. And then he did."

Beat.

My parents liked Billy. They called him "The Suitor". They call Jack "The Plague", because when I first started dating him, I came home with a venereal infection. But it wasn't his fault. He didn't know he had it. And besides, it was the curable kind.

AMANDA *heads offstage after* **BILLY**.

MOVEMENT FOUR: TRUE LOVE

BILLY *and* **AMANDA***, enter, having just climbed up a steep slope that brings them into a wintry orchard.*

AMANDA. I dream of this orchard. Still.

BILLY. I'm not surprised. It's haunting. Especially in the winter. Did I ever bring you here in the winter?

AMANDA. I don't think so. I've never seen it so naked.

BILLY. Yeah, I only came by myself in the winter. It was my special place. I would come here when my Dad was in a particularly bad mood.

AMANDA. (*lost in her own reverie*) When I was fourteen I wanted to marry you here. In the orchard. I wanted a big party with everyone we knew in tuxedos and long feathered gowns. And we'd have an apple cake. And toast with apple brandy. And waltz the whole night away through the apple trees.

BILLY. Do you remember what you used to say to me when we said goodnight?

AMANDA. I'm not sure –

BILLY. You would say "Dream about me." And I would say / "I always do"

AMANDA. (*remembering, with* **BILLY.**) "I always do."

AMANDA *and* **BILLY** *smile at each other. Will they kiss?* **BILLY** *leans in.*

AMANDA. What's bad?

BILLY. Sorry?

AMANDA. You said you would only come here when your Dad was in a particularly –

BILLY. Oh, I don't know. Bad. Drunk. Breaking things. Hitting my mom.

AMANDA. (*amazed*) I never knew that.

BILLY *shrugs.*

BILLY. It was a secret.

AMANDA. This was happening in high school? While we

were dating?

BILLY *nods.*

AMANDA. Why didn't you tell me?

BILLY. Why would I tell you?

AMANDA. I could have helped.

BILLY. Maybe you could have. But all I really wanted back then, was to sleep with you, and I thought if you knew my life wasn't perfect, you wouldn't let me, so –

AMANDA. (*kindly*) I wouldn't have let you anyhow.

BILLY. I know that now. But at fourteen – the possibilities were endless.

Pause. **AMANDA** *stares at* **BILLY.**

AMANDA. Where is he now?

BILLY. My Dad? At home with my mom.

AMANDA. Does he still –

BILLY. No, he takes thorazine now. He's a very different person. Almost sweet.

AMANDA. What's thorazine?

BILLY. It's an anti-psychotic.

AMANDA. Is he –

BILLY. He might be. It's hereditary. Comes out in the late teens or early twenties. I think I'm over the hump but if I start acting strangely, just throw something at my head.

BILLY *smiles at* **AMANDA.** *She looks upset.*

BILLY. It's okay. I'm kidding.

AMANDA. (*deliberately changing the subject*) How's the postal service?

BILLY. Wonderful.

AMANDA *laughs.* **BILLY** *just stares at her.* **AMANDA** *stops.*

AMANDA. Was that a joke?

BILLY. It's a great job. I get to ride around all day and deliver people happy thoughts and presents and good wishes.

AMANDA. And bills.

BILLY. I'm very careful not to put the bills on top. I find the one personal letter and I make sure that's the first thing my client sees.

AMANDA. What if they don't have any personal letters?

BILLY. Then I wait a few days, until they do. And if nothing comes, I write my own.

AMANDA. You write people mail?

BILLY. Sure. Just a little card. Something that says "I'm still thinking about you. I haven't forgotten. Your friend."

AMANDA. Your friend who?

BILLY. That's it. Just "your friend."

AMANDA. And nobody goes to the post office and asks where the fuck their letter came from?

BILLY. Hasn't happened so far.

AMANDA. This place is so weird.

BILLY. How's life on the outside?

AMANDA. It's very exciting.

BILLY. You must have an impressive career by now.

AMANDA. I'm not sure how impressive you'd find it, but I like it.

BILLY. Are you kidding? To make your living as an artist – doing what you love? Bringing new music into the world? I'd say that was pretty impressive.

AMANDA. And I'd agree, but that's not what I do for a living. I'm in advertising.

BILLY. Oh, I – I always assumed you'd stay with music –

AMANDA. I did. I'm in musical advertising.

BILLY. Oh.

AMANDA. Like jingles, for commercials and stuff, I write them.

BILLY. Oh.

AMANDA. You know, like those little songs that you think of when you think of certain products.

BILLY. Wow, some of those songs are really …annoying.

Beat.

AMANDA. Well, sometimes that's the point.

BILLY. Yeah?

AMANDA. So they get stuck in your head.

BILLY. Sneaky. So what happened?

AMANDA. What happened?

BILLY. You left town when we were what, like seventeen, to go to music school. We all thought you were going to be somebody great.

AMANDA. It's not that easy.

BILLY. But you were special.

AMANDA. There's a lot of special people in the world, Billy. Some of them are much more special than me.

BILLY. You met some people that were better than you.

AMANDA. Yeah, quite a few.

BILLY. So you stopped?

AMANDA. Not exactly. I took a sort of break – What??

> **BILLY** *is shaking his head and laughing softly.*

BILLY. Nothing, I just – I think I should have tried a little harder to sleep with you.

AMANDA. WHAT??

BILLY. Your convictions seemed so strong at the time. If I had known you were so full of shit.

AMANDA. You ride around in a postal truck. You live on the same street as my parents. You have never left the town you were born in.

BILLY. I went to college.

AMANDA. You didn't finish.

BILLY. It wasn't for me. But you – all you ever talked about was music school. Being a composer. Traveling the world –

AMANDA. Hey Billy? If you brought me up here to catalog my dreams deferred, don't bother. I know what they are. I'm the one that let them go –

Beat. **BILLY** *looks at* **AMANDA** *sadly.*

AMANDA. I mean – put them on hold.

BILLY. Why?

> **AMANDA** *doesn't say anything for a moment. Stares out over the frozen apples.*

AMANDA. Because I didn't want to be a bitch, Billy. Nobody sees a girl alone with an oboe and thinks she must be brilliant. They think she must be weird or maladjusted or stuck-up. I wanted people to like me. You get all these perks when you're a girl and people like you. You can open doors with a smile. Eventually I realized that those doors don't open very far at all, and besides that, they're the wrong doors and besides that, I didn't even know what doors I should be looking for, because I was too busy watching the boys when they gave that lecture in class. Because *there seemed to be a time crunch.* And a limited supply. And everyone else was getting one –

BILLY. Nobody got me.

AMANDA. So I started to think I'd better get one too. And I did. A great one. A real catch. But it wasn't easy getting him. Because a lot of people wanted him. And it won't be easy keeping him, no matter how much he loves me...

I began thinking, recently ... I have a few years now. Before Jack's career takes off ... before children ... of relative security. I could really get something done. But when I look around for the doors I've been meaning to open...

There used to be doors everywhere. But – it's like, I've forgotten what a door looks like.

God! I'm not making any sense am I?

BILLY. I can show you a door if you'd like.

AMANDA. Can I tell you something totally insane?

Sometimes, I have this feeling that English isn't my first language. Like, I have these thoughts in my head and I don't have the words to put to them. Or I don't know what order to put the words in. And I just know, if I tried to say them aloud, they would sound *crazy*.

BILLY. Ah, now that makes sense.

AMANDA. Very funny.

BILLY. I was a double-major in college before I quit. Linguistics and women's studies.

AMANDA. Don't make fun of me please.

BILLY. And I studied language. How it's constructed. It turns out, most languages, most western languages, operate on a system of binary oppositions. Everything has an opposite. So you've got black and white, good and evil, rich and poor ... man and woman. And, because our language shapes our consciousness, the way we instinctually understand something is by its relationship to its opposite. But the fucked up thing is, those binaries are calibrated. Meaning, one side is the standard and its opposite is *lacking* the standard. So black is lacking white. Poor is lacking rich. Woman is lacking man.

This makes sense because our western languages are derivations of Latin and Rome was an epicenter of rich, white men. But it leaves women and non-white people sort of out in the cold.

I learned in my women's studies courses that Virginia Woolf had a theory about a female sentence versus a male sentence. A male sentence is aggressive. Linear. It has an objective and, when it communicates that objective, the sentence is over. A female sentence is more circuitous. The point is not necessarily to achieve, but rather to explore. To convey feeling. Mental state. Consciousness. Images. Like Woolf's novels. The problem is – you can't read too many female sentences in a row or you feel like you're going insane. There's no order there. Nothing happens. They keep looping over and under themselves, forward and backwards. I hated reading Woolf. I thought it was a waste of time.

But my professor had a good point. She said that there was order in the writing, but it wasn't the order we expected. It wasn't the system we had learned. The writer was tapping a consciousness that did not have a language. Which is why, all of this has been a very long way of crediting your feelings about speaking in a foreign tongue. You might be right. Our language, the language we speak, might not be your first language. As a woman.

Pause.

BILLY. I'm done.

AMANDA. Are you sure?

BILLY. I'm sure. I just told you everything I ever learned in college. I'm done.

AMANDA just stares at him.

BILLY. Bullshit, right? I thought so too, at first, but I'm telling you, it makes sense if you –

AMANDA kisses BILLY.

AMANDA. Oh my god.

BILLY doesn't answer. Waits.

AMANDA. I just kissed you.

BILLY nods. Waits.

AMANDA. I'm getting married.

BILLY nods again. Waits.

AMANDA. To someone else!

BILLY kisses AMANDA.

AMANDA. I have to go.

AMANDA stands.

AMANDA. Why didn't you tell me you were so smart? In high school?

BILLY. I wasn't this smart in high school.

AMANDA. You could have really made something of yourself.

BILLY. And then what? You'd be marrying me instead of Bon Jovi? If only you knew I had a brain in my head back in high school. Give me a break.

AMANDA. (*furious at herself*) You're right. I've got no business being here. I have some weird case of cold feet and it's making me delusional. I've got a fiancée back in New York who is very good-looking and about to be embarrassingly successful and all I have to do is get in the car and drive back to the city and when I wake up tomorrow this will all be one of those stupid orchard dreams I've had a million times. Nothing more.

BILLY. Okay. It was nice to see you again.

AMANDA. Okay. So long.

AMANDA turns and starts to walk away. She stops. She starts again. She stops again. She turns around.

AMANDA. You're not going to even try and stop me?

BILLY. Nope.

AMANDA. This is it, Billy. Your second chance. Your *only* second chance. Most people never even get this.

BILLY. I know what this is.

AMANDA. Well you're fucking it up royally.

BILLY. I know what I'm doing.

AMANDA. Fine.

BILLY. Alright.

AMANDA. See you NEVER AGAIN.

BILLY. Good-bye.

AMANDA turns and walks off-stage.

Beat.

Beat.

AMANDA comes back on stage. She walks right up to BILLY. Stops in front of him.

AMANDA. Would you like to have sex with me?

BILLY. Yes.

AMANDA. Now?

BILLY. Sure.

AMANDA. Here?

BILLY. Fine.

> **BILLY** *kisses* **AMANDA**.

AMANDA. Tomorrow, this means nothing.

BILLY. Agreed.

> **BILLY** *kisses* **AMANDA** *again. The kissing becomes more passionate.*

AMANDA. Billy?

BILLY. Hmm?

AMANDA. When I slapped you earlier – I meant that for someone else. Maybe everyone else.

BILLY. I know.

AMANDA. How did you know?

BILLY. I know you.

> *They continue kissing. Lights down. The orchard disappears.*

MOVEMENT FIVE: INDEPENDENCE

Lights up. **KIM** *is sitting on a pile of suitcases. She's on the phone. Around her,* **DAVID** *and* **BILLY** *bring on the New Hampshire apartment.*

KIM. No, I didn't ask my shrink … Because he gets some exorbitant sum of money to talk to me every week so that David doesn't have to. He's not going to advise me to follow my dreams – … Yes, I have dreams Carol … I can't remember what they are anymore, that's why I have to leave – … Look Carol, you're my goddamn sister, I shouldn't have to justify myself to you. Just change the motherfucking sheets.

AMANDA *enters.*

KIM. Carol, my wayward daughter just came home. You may be off the hook. I'll call you later … You can't say that, I'm your sister.

KIM *hangs up the phone.*

KIM. (*to* **AMANDA**) Where the hell have you been?
AMANDA. Are we still packing or are we done?
KIM. I've been worried sick. Oh my God –
AMANDA. Because, if we're done –
KIM. I know that face.
AMANDA. I have to get back –
KIM. You just got laid.

Beat.

AMANDA. I'd like to beat the traffic.
KIM. That's your I-just-got-laid face.
AMANDA. And you have a remarkable amount of unpacking to do before Daddy gets home.
KIM. That's the face you used to make in high school.
AMANDA. I never got laid in high school Mom.
KIM. I knew what you and Billy Theebles were up to every

time you went "apple-picking".

AMANDA. We were apple-picking.

KIM. You might be the only person who got laid last night in this entire town. You should be congratulated. Well, really Billy should be congratulated.

AMANDA. Tell me you didn't follow me.

KIM. I didn't follow you.

AMANDA. Then how did you know I spent the night with Billy?

KIM. Instead I utilized my highly rarified system of specialized spy technology. I like to call it –

KIM goes over to the window and draws back the curtain.

KIM. Operation curtains. So how was he?

AMANDA. Mom –

KIM. Better than high school?

AMANDA. I didn't sleep with him in high school.

KIM. Why not?

AMANDA. I wasn't supposed to –

KIM. You never did anything you weren't supposed to. The whole reason I had a kid was to add a little excitement into my life. But instead I got you. It was like raising my mother.

AMANDA. (*coldly*) I'm sorry that life hasn't turned out the way you wanted it to Mom.

KIM. (*equally cold*) Save your sympathy. Wait your turn.

AMANDA. When is Dad coming home?

KIM. A couple of hours.

AMANDA. Do you want me to help you unpack now?

KIM. I'M LEAVING HIM!

AMANDA. WHY?

KIM. He's having an affair.

AMANDA. You don't know that –

KIM. I found underwear in his jacket pocket.

AMANDA. Maybe somebody slipped it into his pocket at work. As a practical joke. To get him in trouble with his wife. You should at least ask him.

KIM. I'll call him from your place in New York and ask him.

AMANDA. You've been married thirty years. You owe him an explanation. Out of respect for –

KIM. For what? Time?

AMANDA. For him.

KIM. Oh him. (*Mini-beat*). No. Let's go.

AMANDA. Go?

KIM. You're taking me to New York.

AMANDA. No, Mom, I'm not. One of us has to be the responsible one in this circumstance and as usual, it looks like it has to be me –

KIM. Responsible for who?

AMANDA. For Dad. And for you. For the sanctity of your union.

KIM. For the sanctity of our – my God, the things that sound reasonable when you're twenty-five.

AMANDA. Give me one good reason why you should leave my father.

KIM. And then you'll drive me to New York?

AMANDA. Fine.

Beat.

KIM. I'm tired of cooking.

AMANDA. I'm leaving. You're staying.

AMANDA *picks up her bags and starts out the door.*

KIM. You said if I gave you one –

AMANDA. That is not a good reason.

KIM. I think it is.

AMANDA. Take the train.

KIM. I'm not dead yet.

AMANDA *turns around.*

AMANDA. What?

KIM. There – that's two good reasons. I get to drive.

AMANDA. Mom –

KIM. Marriage is a contract Amanda, not a sacred union. And the reason I signed it and the reason you're going to sign it is because when you're a young woman it seems like a good idea. Because the world seems huge and foreign and full of rapists and nobody takes you seriously. The trouble is, after you're married, not only do they not take you seriously – they're not even *curious* anymore. But nobody tells you that.

AMANDA. People take me seriously. I'm good at what I do.

KIM. I told you that you could have everything. That you never had to compromise. My generation made all the compromises for you. I feel bad about that. That wasn't something I *knew,* per se. Just something I was hoping would come true.

AMANDA. Don't worry about me. I'll figure it out.

KIM. Not if you marry Jack Handel.

AMANDA. Do you know how many girls out there would kill to marry Jack Handel?

KIM. So let one of them. Not you. You go live a life.

AMANDA. There are happily married women in the world Mom! Just because you couldn't make it work –

KIM. I am a happily married woman! I'm telling you – it's a farce. Your kids will leave you – your husband will leave you – it's natural – everybody dies alone. But you – you have the opportunity to leave something truly extraordinary behind. You're throwing it all away before you've even tried.

AMANDA. It's not that easy. I could try to do this my whole life and never get anywhere at it. And if I walk away from Jack, I will walk away from an extraordinary life.

KIM. No! Jack will have an extraordinary life. And because of that, he's going to be difficult and demanding, his head will swell, he'll fuck around, and you'll stay home, raise his kids and worry about contracting herpes from your husband.

Beat. **AMANDA** *stares at* **KIM**.

AMANDA. When did you become such a bitch?

KIM. I don't know. It just happened. I woke up one morning and discovered black hairs growing above my lip. And I thought, "Well, there goes your smile, old girl. You can either give up now or learn to fight like a dog." It's not so bad actually. I never did get anything I really wanted with a smile.

AMANDA. That's just menopause. It's totally normal.

KIM. It's *wonderful*. I'm producing testosterone for the first time in my life. My head is so clear. I want to do something with myself. I want to hunt for something and find it and break it. I want to build something huge and complex and ugly. I want to win an argument. Before I die. Using logic! I want to scream at someone and make them cry and *feel good* about it.

AMANDA. (*getting mad*) This is really shitty timing Kim. I think you know that. I think you planned it this way.

KIM. (*even madder*) We cannot both be housewives. If you marry Jack, I have to leave your father. One of us needs to live an extraordinary life.

Beat. **AMANDA** *turns away.*

KIM. Are you crying?

AMANDA. No.

KIM *looks closely at* **AMANDA**.

KIM. Yes, you are. I don't feel good about that. Damn. What is the matter with me? Shit.

A concession.

If it will make you feel better, I won't leave your father until after you marry Jack.

AMANDA. That doesn't make me feel better.

KIM. It's a good offer. You should take it.

AMANDA stares at her mother.

She notices a painting among the stuff that her mother packed.

AMANDA. Why are you taking that painting? Is it worth something?

KIM. No, I just like it.

AMANDA. It looks vaguely famous.

KIM. It's worthless. Just sentimental.

AMANDA. Have you ever had it appraised?

KIM. No.

AMANDA. Where did you get it?

KIM. I painted it.

AMANDA. What?

KIM. I painted it.

Beat.

You don't have to believe me. I'd understand.

AMANDA looks more closely at the painting.

AMANDA. Is that you?

KIM. Yes.

AMANDA. How old were you?

KIM. Young. Your age.

AMANDA. I thought you worked at an art gallery when you were my age.

KIM. I did.

AMANDA. You mean you *sold your work* at an art gallery?

KIM. Right.

AMANDA. You never told me that.

KIM. You never asked.

AMANDA. Why the hell did you give it up? This is really good.

Beat.

KIM. It all started to seem a little silly after a while. I had a husband and a child. What was I supposed to do – put you in front of the television so I could go paint? What kind of a mother does that?

KIM takes the painting from AMANDA and looks at it.

I knew I would never paint anything as beautiful as you.

Silence.

AMANDA. You really think I'm making a huge mistake?

KIM. It's not the choice I would have made if I had it to do over again.

AMANDA. What would you do instead?

KIM. (*getting emotional*) I would take an easel to a mountain somewhere, set it up on the edge of a cliff, mix my paints, stare at the horizon and try to live forever.

KIM looks at the painting one more time, then hands it back. She gets up and starts to exit.

AMANDA. Where are you going?

KIM. Since we've decided that I'm not leaving your father tonight, I'm going upstairs. I tivoed Desperate Housewives.

AMANDA. What should I do now?

KIM. What do you want to do sweetheart?

AMANDA. Disappear.

KIM. And I just want to be seen. See? It's rigged.

KIM leaves the room. AMANDA thinks for a moment.

Then she grabs her coat and heads out the door.

Lights down.

MOVEMENT SIX: A SIMPLE LIFE

Lights up outside another door. **BILLY***'s.* **AMANDA**
knocks. **BILLY** *opens the door in his pajamas.*

BILLY. Amanda?

AMANDA. I want to try something.

BILLY. Okay. What?

AMANDA. This.

> **AMANDA** *kisses* **BILLY**.

AMANDA. How was that?

BILLY. Nice.

AMANDA. And this.

> **AMANDA** *kisses* **BILLY** *again.*

BILLY. That was nice too.

AMANDA. And what about this?

> **AMANDA** *takes* **BILLY***'s hand.*

BILLY. What are you doing?

AMANDA. How does this feel?

BILLY. (*warily*) Nice.

AMANDA. Don't you want to invite me in?

BILLY. Why?

AMANDA. I want to try something else.

BILLY. (*smiling*) What?

AMANDA. I think you should invite me in.

BILLY. (*teasing*) What do you want to try?

> *Beat.*

AMANDA. I think we've got something here, don't you?

BILLY. Uh-huh.

AMANDA. A real connection, right?

BILLY. I guess so.

AMANDA. There's something about the people who knew

you when you were young – before you had decided
who you wanted to be. Before you knew what face you
wanted to wear in the world. They're the only ones
who really know you, you know?

BILLY. Sure.

AMANDA. You knew that I wasn't going to leave you in the
apple orchard. You knew that I would come back,
right?

BILLY. Yeah.

AMANDA. How did you know?

BILLY. You like boys who play hard to get. At least you did
back in high school.

AMANDA. Exactly! I do. I don't like to feel forced. I like to
make my own decisions.

BILLY. That's not what I said. I said you like to chase
people.

AMANDA. Whatever. The point is you – get me. You really
get me. More than anyone ever has. More than anyone
ever will.

BILLY. Okay.

AMANDA. So what do you think?

BILLY. I'm sorry. I'm having a hard time following this conversation. I'm a little stoned.

AMANDA. (*thrown*) Oh. That's okay.

In fact …

That's *exactly* why I like you. Because you're stoned
right now. Because *you get stoned.*

BILLY. I get stoned.

AMANDA. You get stoned. And you're chill and you're sweet
and you love me just the way I am. And you have a
government job, which means the hours are very reasonable, so you'll be able to pick up our son from
soccer and drop our daughter at ballet –

BILLY. Who?

AMANDA. And I'll bet you're a half-decent cook, aren't you?
And you'll never have money. But I don't want money.

I just want love and companionship and the chance to be fulfilled artistically. You can have it all! You just can't have it all and be rich. But you're much smarter than I ever thought, which means our children will turn out smart, which means they can get themselves scholarships – can I come in?

BILLY. Hold up –

AMANDA. What's the matter?

BILLY. Hold-the-hell-up.

AMANDA. Okay. I'm holding –

BILLY. SLOW THE FUCK DOWN.

AMANDA. Billy! It's okay. I'm done.

BILLY. You've stopped?

AMANDA. I've stopped.

BILLY. Okay. I just need a moment here. To process some information.

Beat.

BILLY. Are you pregnant?

AMANDA. From last night? I don't think so.

BILLY. We used a condom, right?

AMANDA. Yes.

BILLY. Okay good, that's what I thought. Okay. So, why are you here?

AMANDA. Billy!

BILLY. That's me.

AMANDA. I want to try a relationship. With you.

BILLY. What sort of relationship?

AMANDA. A permanent one.

BILLY. A permanent one. Yeah. Okay. I should say that I'm flattered. I'm very, very flattered. But I don't think I'm in a place in my life right now where I can be very generous to anybody else.

AMANDA. What?

BILLY. But I like you a whole lot. And I'm really glad we had the opportunity to reestablish contact.

AMANDA. WHAT?

BILLY. And I'd like us to remain friends. I mean – if that's cool with you.

AMANDA. What about last night?

BILLY. Last night was awesome.

AMANDA. All the things we said to each other.

BILLY. It was intense.

AMANDA. You told me all women were forced to speak the language of their oppressors.

BILLY. No, I said that most dominant western languages are constructed on a hierarchical system of binary opposites that implies the innate inferiority of women. You can speak whatever you want. You don't have to speak at all.

AMANDA. I thought you loved me.

BILLY. (*honestly bewildered*) Did I say that?

AMANDA. Why did you sleep with me, then?

BILLY. You asked me to.

AMANDA. Bullshit. You brought me up there to … bed me.

BILLY. Bed?

AMANDA. Fuck!

BILLY. Well yes –

AMANDA. WHY?

BILLY. Are you kidding? You left me with blue-balls through my entire adolescence. I've been waiting to fuck you for ten years. That's the longest time I've ever wanted anything. I don't know what I'm going to do with the *rest* of my life. That's what I was thinking about today when I decided to get high.

AMANDA *stares at* BILLY *for a second.*

BILLY. Come on. You really want to move back to New Hampshire and bear the fruit of my loins? Amanda Blue, you were going to be huge.

AMANDA *turns and walks off, leaving* BILLY *alone*

onstage. Lights down.

MOVEMENT 7: OBLIVION

Lights up in **KIM**'s *house.* **AMANDA** *enters. There's nobody there.* **KIM**'s *suitcases are gone.*

AMANDA. Mom? Kim?

DAVID, *Amanda's father, enters, reading some pages of computer print-outs on perforated paper. He has a glass of brandy in his hand.*

DAVID. Hello Kitty.

AMANDA. Dad? What are you doing here?

DAVID. I live here. What are you doing here? Hiding out?

AMANDA. Mom called. She … she needed my help with something. Is she here?

DAVID. I haven't seen her. I was hoping there'd be something for me to eat when I got home. But no such luck. I was just about to order a pizza. Care to join me?

AMANDA searches room. **DAVID** *sits down on the couch, absorbed in his reading.*

What are you looking for?

AMANDA. She didn't leave a note or anything?

DAVID. (*not looking up*) She's probably at another one of her classes. She's been taking night classes at the community college.

AMANDA. Why?

DAVID. I suppose my conversation is not that stimulating anymore.

Looking up, he clocks **AMANDA**'s *face.*

DAVID. Oh Kitty, I don't take it personally – when you get to be our age you need a little new information every now and then. Wards off Alzheimers.

AMANDA. What are you reading?

DAVID. Oh this? It's my new hobby.

AMANDA. Those pages are perforated.

DAVID. They come out of the printer like that.

AMANDA. *What is wrong with New Hampshire?*

DAVID. (*pleased*) It's like reading a scroll.

AMANDA. What's your new hobby Dad?

DAVID. Well I discovered recently that, at the college library, they have periodicals, on microfiche, that go all the way back to the middle of the 19th century. I spent a whole month reading the New York Times from October 1929, right around the time the stock market crashed. You'll never guess what dominated the headlines the morning of the crash.

AMANDA opens her mouth to respond. DAVID beats her to the punch.

A transatlantic call Edison made to Einstein. They were celebrating the miracle of *that* technology for three days. The story of the stock fall was buried on page 16. It took the New York Times three days to realize that anything was seriously wrong. Why am I fascinated by this?

Again, AMANDA tries to speak – again, she's too slow.

As I get older I'm becoming aware of the paradox of existence. What do I mean by this? Well, it occurred to me some time ago that, despite my mental acuity, I was no longer a young man. That I am growing continuously older. That aging is not a definite process but rather a fundament of life. Though I consider myself eighteen, I am the only one. I am perceived as older by others and thus must adjust my behavior to accommodate this new reality. But no sooner have I learned to act, say thirty, but I am already fifty and must adapt again. Is that a paradox?

AMANDA just shrugs.

No, that is clearly not a paradox. The paradox lies in comparing my life of perpetual dynamism with the stasis of humanity as a whole. What does this have to do with newspaper archives?

AMANDA *puts a pillow over her head.* **DAVID** *keeps talking.*

Well by reading these first hand accounts of human history, I have come to the conclusion that, as a species, we are fundamentally no different then we were seventy-five years ago. The world has gotten older but we are still hanging by our teeth from a frayed rope above the mouth of anarchy ... I read that in an editorial from 1929.

AMANDA. (*lowering the pillow*) Dad?

DAVID. Yes?

AMANDA. I'm glad you've found something that interests you.

DAVID. It's important. I've been bored.

AMANDA. (*an accusation*) Why don't you go with Mom to her classes?

DAVID. Your mother and I have already spent quite a bit of time together.

AMANDA. But you love each other.

DAVID. Even still, when you've been married to someone as long as your mother and I have been married, you'll understand. After a while it's not so different from spending time with yourself.

AMANDA. What's wrong with that?

DAVID. We know ourselves well. There are a lot of other people in the world that I would like to get to know.

AMANDA. Is that why you're spending your time reading newspapers from 1929?

DAVID. It's more social than you think. I have a very nice lady friend there, a librarian, who helps me out quite a bit.

AMANDA. She's a librarian?!

DAVID. Yes, and a part-time figure skater if you can believe it. The library is sort of her day job. Apparently competitive figure skating is very expensive. Especially if you aren't very good.

AMANDA. I can't believe you're telling me this.

DAVID. Not interested, huh? That's too bad. I thought now that you were older we could be friends. Am I disappointed? I suppose slightly. But part me is pleased that I can still think of you as a self-obsessed adolescent. Then I must not be very old either.

AMANDA. Dad, I have something I have to say to you –

DAVID. Where is your mother? I'd be more comfortable if you said it to her and then she translated it to me.

AMANDA. She's gone.

DAVID. Perhaps you could wait until she returns to issue your manifesto.

AMANDA. She's not coming back. She's gone for good. She left you.

Beat.

DAVID. That isn't nice Amanda.

AMANDA. It's the truth Dad.

DAVID gets up abruptly and goes out of the room. He comes back a moment later, his face ashen. He sits down.

DAVID. She took my favorite painting.

AMANDA. Dad –

DAVID. Are you staying here tonight?

AMANDA. Do you want me to?

DAVID. You must be anxious to get back to the city.

AMANDA. I'd rather stay here tonight. Unless you want to invite someone else over.

DAVID. Who?

Beat.

DAVID. I don't have any friends. Your mother has friends.

Silence.

DAVID. Your mother tells me you're planning a wedding.

AMANDA. Technically Jack's manager is planning a wedding. But I am engaged.

DAVID. That calls for a toast.

> **DAVID** *goes to a cabinet beneath the bookcases and pulls out a bottle of wine.*

DAVID. I've been saving this.

AMANDA. (*reading the label*) Handel Vineyards?

DAVID. It's from a small winery near Toronto. I picked it up on a business trip. On the night before you marry Jack Handel, I was planning to open up this bottle of wine and drink myself into oblivion.

Beat.

DAVID. But might as well drink it now.

AMANDA. Doesn't anybody like Jack?

DAVID. Theoretically you do, Kitty.

AMANDA. He's not a bad person.

DAVID. Certainly not. If you're partial to pretentious little farts.

> **AMANDA** *stares at him. She's tired of defending herself to everyone.*

AMANDA. I am so sad. Why am I so sad? I'm too young to be sad.

DAVID. You're not sad. I'm sad. You're just scared.

AMANDA. You don't know what I'm talking about.

DAVID. I was young once too.

AMANDA. But you were a young man. It's not the same thing.

DAVID. You think people don't take seriously because you're a woman.

AMANDA. It isn't fair.

DAVID. Life isn't fair.

AMANDA. Thanks Dad.

DAVID. Luckily, it's not very long. And nothing that you do matters.

AMANDA. You don't even take me seriously.

DAVID. I do take you seriously. I took your mother seriously when she came to the same conclusion thirty years ago. I don't know what to tell you, Kitty. That's just the way it is.

AMANDA. That isn't helpful.

DAVID. Jesus Amanda, put your life in perspective. Thirty percent of Africa is dying of AIDS.

AMANDA. You don't believe this is a real problem.

DAVID. I think there are a lot of people in the world who don't feel appreciated for who they are. For example, I seriously doubt your mother appreciates me very much right now despite the fact that I've shown that woman nothing but love for thirty years.

AMANDA. Until you started sleeping with a librarian.

Beat.

DAVID. Is that what she told you?

AMANDA. She knows you're having an affair, Dad. That's why she left.

DAVID. That's not possible.

AMANDA. What's not possible? The fact that she found out or the fact that she left you over it?

DAVID. The "fact that she found out" is actually the part that's perplexing me.

AMANDA. She found someone's underwear in your coat pocket.

DAVID. Did she? May I see said underwear?

AMANDA *hesitates.*

DAVID. I can – I can only imagine what you think of me right now.

AMANDA *exits and returns with the underwear wrapped*

in tinfoil. She hands it silently to her father. He unwraps the package and lifts out its contents.

DAVID. These are your mother's.

AMANDA. (*disgusted*) Dad.

DAVID. I bought them for her, years ago. When we were first married. As a sort of joke. I thought she had thrown them out.

AMANDA. I don't believe you.

DAVID. I honestly don't care. I have other problems right now.

AMANDA. Why would she put her underwear in your coat pocket and tell me it belonged to the woman you were sleeping with?

DAVID. It does belong to the woman I am sleeping with –

AMANDA. She said you were having an affair!

DAVID. I suppose she wanted to believe I was.

AMANDA. Why?

DAVID. Isn't it obvious?

AMANDA. No! Why would she leave you if she didn't have to?

DAVID. She wants to leave me, Amanda. She's been waiting for an excuse. She must be tired of waiting.

AMANDA. So she made up a reason?

DAVID *shrugs.*

AMANDA. That's insane.

DAVID. Really? May I suggest you're marrying Jack Handel because you can't find a good reason why you shouldn't marry Jack Handel.

AMANDA. What does it matter? If it doesn't work out, I can just stuff my underwear in his pocket and walk out the door.

DAVID. I doubt it was that easy. But yes, you now have that option. And that is what has changed from my generation to yours. It took your mother thirty years do this. It will take you three.

AMANDA. This doesn't make any sense.

DAVID. What?

AMANDA. Any of it!

DAVID. Some of it makes sense. I find the seasons to be relatively consistent. Thunder follows lightening. Heat melts snow. That's the sort of causality you can hang your hat on.

AMANDA. Nothing makes sense to me but music.

DAVID. So go there.

AMANDA. Name a female composer. Name one.

DAVID. I can't.

AMANDA. You see?

DAVID. Amanda, I can't name any composer more contemporary than Gershwin.

AMANDA. They're hard to find. In graduate school, I was in a class with four men. All my teachers were men. By the second year I started having a recurring dream. I'm at a party with all my classmates and somehow I've ended up as the hostess. In walks a young Wolfgang Amadeus. He comes up to me, he kisses me on both cheeks and he says "Amanda, ma cherie, please do me the honor of introducing me to my competition". He means my classmates, Dad. The boys. But before I've finished, Johannes Bach walks in, kisses me on both cheeks and requests an introduction. And fast on his heels are coming Beethoven, Shubert, Chopin and Wagner. I turn around and I am attacked by Tchaikovsky, Bernstein, Copeland, Gershwin. I have just become a conduit between famous men, a facilitator of introductions, a vessel for the communication between genius and genius. And I find myself becoming more and more agitated because I have this feeling that someone is missing. But I can see that everyone who matters is already there.

I'm not making this up Dad.

DAVID. I know you're not Kitty.

AMANDA. I don't know what I'm supposed to do about it.

DAVID. There's not much you can do about it.

AMANDA. I want to be a great composer.

DAVID. So write great music.

AMANDA. I DON'T HAVE TIME. I have a full-time job. I have a fiancée to love. I have a mother, newly single, who I have to look after. I have you to worry about. I have to make dinner. I have a bathroom that gets dirty. I sound like an idiot. – What are you doing?

DAVID *is stuffing the underwear into the pocket of Amanda's jacket.*

AMANDA. What are you doing? Dad!

DAVID. There.

AMANDA. What?

DAVID. There's your excuse.

AMANDA *takes the underwear out and stares at them.*

DAVID. You can use it now. Or you can wrap it in tinfoil and put it back in the refrigerator for another thirty years. It will always be there. Waiting for you.

AMANDA *doesn't know what to say.*

DAVID. There is one significant difference between you and Bach and Beethoven.

Those men are dead.

AMANDA. (*the real fear*) What if I'm not good enough?

DAVID. You'll die too.

AMANDA. I'm serious –

DAVID. But if you are good enough – if you're so good, you exceed everyone's wildest expectations – same deal.

Beat.

Do you want me to put them back in the refrigerator?

AMANDA *thinks about it for a moment.*

AMANDA. I'll keep them.

DAVID. You sure? Because I'm going to the kitchen now.

I'm on my way there. I'm going to unload the dish-washer, so it wouldn't be any trouble at all to make a quick stopover at the refrigerator –

AMANDA. I'm SURE.

DAVID. Good. I'm glad you're sure.

AMANDA. Dad?

DAVID. Kitty?

AMANDA. Mom's gone.

DAVID. I'm beginning to understand that.

AMANDA. Why are you so calm?

> **DAVID** *considers this.*

DAVID. What should I do?

> **DAVID** *waits. A genuine question.*

AMANDA. I don't know.

> **DAVID** *smiles, very sad.*

DAVID. I think she'll be back. The world is not particularly kind to women over fifty.

> **DAVID** *exits calmly into the kitchen.* **AMANDA** *sits down on the couch, staring at the underwear.*
>
> *All of the sudden, a terrible crashing sound is heard. Followed by another and another.* **AMANDA** *jumps up and goes to the doorway.*

AMANDA. Dad?

> *A plate is hurled through the doorway. It shatters at* **AMANDA**'*s feet. She jumps back.*
>
> *Lights down.*

DA CAPO: TO BEGIN AGAIN AT THE BEGINNING.

Lights up. **AMANDA** *is front and center, downstage. She clutches the underwear in her hand. Behind her,* **BILLY** *and* **DAVID** *are carrying all the furniture and scenery off stage.*

AMANDA. (*to the audience*) I'm sorry that I left you back there. I got a little overwhelmed. Things didn't happen the way I expected them to.

I'm back in New York. This is the door to my apartment.

AMANDA *fishes the key out of her bag.*

AMANDA. I slept at my parents' house last night. Or maybe it's my father's house now. I don't know. I helped him sweep up all the broken China. We ordered Chinese food and ate it off of paper plates. He didn't say much else for the rest of the night. When I left this morning he was still in bed.

I don't know where my mother is.

It's strange to think I used to have a family. Like I used to have a dog. Or I used to have short hair. Separated, the parts don't add up to anything. We're just people now.

AMANDA *sighs. Turns to the apartment. Turns back.*

AMANDA. What if Jack is inside fucking his manager?

AMANDA *knocks. Jack opens the door.*

JACK. Hi.

AMANDA. Hi.

JACK. You got a letter. From the New York Symphonique.

JACK *hands* **AMANDA** *the letter. She opens it. Reads.*

JACK. What does it say?

AMANDA. It says one of my classmates won the spring New

Voices festival.

AMANDA *folds the letter up and puts it back in the envelope.*

AMANDA. I have to tell you something.

JACK. I have to tell you something.

AMANDA. You go first.

JACK. I want a prenup.

AMANDA. I slept with someone else.

AMANDA *takes off her engagement ring and hands it to* **JACK.** *He puts it in his pocket, sadly. He goes back into the apartment. Lights down on* **JACK.**

AMANDA *turns back to the audience. She is finally at a loss for words.*

JACK *reappears and hands her a beautiful, new oboe.*

AMANDA. What's this?

JACK. It's what I should have given you originally.

AMANDA. It's beautiful.

JACK. Yo baby, you gotta be certain. You got the goods. But if you ain't selling, can't nobody be buying.

AMANDA *looks at him, confused by the dialect.*

JACK. I'm breaking into hip-hop.

AMANDA. Good luck with that.

JACK *puts on his shades.*

JACK. I'm going to LA for a while. I'll call you when I come back.

AMANDA *nods.*

Lights down on **JACK.**

AMANDA. (*to the audience*) There's a song I've wanted to write my whole life. It begins with the sounds of snow melting off the roof of the house I grew up in.

The same high, tin notes.

AMANDA. And falling into tin pails, which wakes the sleeping frogs.

The low, croaking chords.

AMANDA. The front door of my house opens with the first burst of sun ... and my mother steps into a wintry morning.

AMANDA's *symphony begins to play.*

AMANDA. Her hair is wet and her cheeks are red. She has a palette in one hand and a paintbrush in the other. And she's pregnant. With me.

My mother's song is... coming. It's coming.

I dreamed the party dream again last night. But this time, there were women everywhere. They appeared dimly at first, like ghosts, moving between the men. Nobody else saw them. But I did. So I excused myself from the circle of introductions. I picked up my oboe and I played. The women danced. And I remember thinking, if I never stop playing, maybe they'll stay.

AMANDA *puts the oboe to her mouth. She lowers it again.*

AMANDA. In music, the term "feminine ending" is used when a phrase or movement ends in an unstressed note or weak cadence.

In literary terminology, the technique is called a "dying rhyme".

I am afraid this is a feminine ending.

I am ... afraid.

AMANDA *puts her lips to the reed and blows a perfect A. As the lights fade, the sound of an orchestra rises, tuning.*

END OF PLAY.

PROPERTY PLOT

WHAT	WHO	NOTES
Oboe	Brooke	
Reed	Brooke	
Keyboard	Brooke	
Mic Stand	Peter	
Wireless Mic		
Earplugs	Peter	
Wireless Phone	Brooke/Amy	
Handset	Amy	Attached to wall
Ring Box	Peter	
Ring	Peter	See Costumes
Cell Phone	Peter	
Thick Envelope	Brooke/Peter	To be opened each show w/ "bloody tampon"
Letter (in thick envelope)	Brooke/Peter	To be opened each show
Extra Mail		In mail bag
Suitcases	Alan/Amy	Alan: Black rollon (1); Amy: Matching set (3)
Suitcase Dressing	Amy	See Costumes
Tissue Paper	Amy	For packing
Pile of Suitcases	Amy	
Bag of white powder	Amy	
Purse	Amy	See Costumes
Tin foil wrapped panties	Amy	Hot pink, lacey panties
Key	Brooke	
Mail Bag	Jedadiah	
Painting	Amy	
Glass of Brandy	Alan	
Print-out from computer	Alan	
Bottle of Wine	Alan	
"Letter from New York Symphonique"	Brooke	
New Oboe		
Pad of Paper w/ Pencil	Brooke	
Handled Shopping Bag	Peter	For "new" shoes
Candle	Amy	Battery Operated
Car Key	Brooke	
Bottle of Brandy	Alan	
Matching Arm Chairs		
Small Table		Between Chairs
Pillow		On chair in New Hampshire
Table	Brooke	For keyboard
Chair	Brooke	For keyboard; metal, diner-type
Murphey Bed Dressing		
Murphey Bed		
Small Pictures		On Piano
Console Piano		New Hampshire setting
Small Lamps		On Piano

Candles		Some for piano; some for table btw. chairs
Wrist Watch	Brooke	
Wrist Watch	Peter	
Earrings	Brooke	
Purse	Amy	
Engagement Ring	Brooke	
"Shoulder Bag"	Brooke	

THE SCENE
Theresa Rebeck

Little Theatre / Drama / 2m, 2f / Interior Unit Set
A young social climber leads an actor into an extra-marital
affair, from which he then creates a full-on downward spiral
into alcoholism and bummery. His wife runs off with his best
friend, his girlfriend leaves, and he's left with… nothing.

"Ms. Rebeck's dark-hued morality tale contains enough fresh
insights into the cultural landscape to freshen what is essen-
tially a classic boy-meets-bad-girl story."
- *New York Times*

"Rebeck's wickedly scathing observations about the sort of
self-obsessed New Yorkers who pursue their own interests at
the cost of their morality and loyalty."
- *New York Post*

"The Scene is utterly delightful in its comedic performances,
and its slowly unraveling plot is thought-provoking and gut-
wrenching."
- *Show Business Weekly*

THE OFFICE PLAYS
Two full length plays by Adam Bock

THE RECEPTIONIST
Comedy / 2m., 2f. Interior

At the start of a typical day in the Northeast Office, Beverly deals effortlessly with ringing phones and her colleague's romantic troubles. But the appearance of a charming rep from the Central Office disrupts the friendly routine. And as the true nature of the company's business becomes apparent, The Receptionist raises disquieting, provocative questions about the consequences of complicity with evil.

"...Mr. Bock's poisoned Post-it note of a play."
- New York Times

"Bock's intense initial focus on the routine goes to the heart of *The Receptionist's* pointed, painfully timely allegory... elliptical, provocative play..."
- Time Out New York

THE THUGS
Comedy / 2m, 6f / Interior

The Obie Award winning dark comedy about work, thunder and the mysterious things that are happening on the 9th floor of a big law firm. When a group of temps try to discover the secrets that lurk in the hidden crevices of their workplace, they realize they would rather believe in gossip and rumors than face dangerous realities.

"Bock starts you off giggling, but leaves you with a chill."
- Time Out New York

"... a delightfully paranoid little nightmare that is both more chillingly realistic and pointedly absurd than anything John Grisham ever dreamed up."
- New York Times

CPSIA information can be obtained
at www.ICGtesting.com
Printed in the USA
LVOW13s0736180417
531067LV00013B/58/P